The Wonderful Number 1

A Birthday Number Book

by Kitty Higgins

Illustrated by Kipling West

**Andrews McMeel
Publishing**

Kansas City

www.andrewsmcmeel.com

The Wonderful Number 1 is produced by becker&mayer!, Ltd.

ISBN: 0-8362-3217-8
Library of Congress Catalog Card Number: 97-70373

Edited by Alison Herschberg
Illustrated by Kipling West
Book design by Simon Sung
Cover design by Heidi Baughman
Cover illustration by Cary Pillo

Happy birthday,
One-year-old,
These pages are just
For you!
Open up the book
And see what
The number one
Can do!

One new tooth.
One big smile.

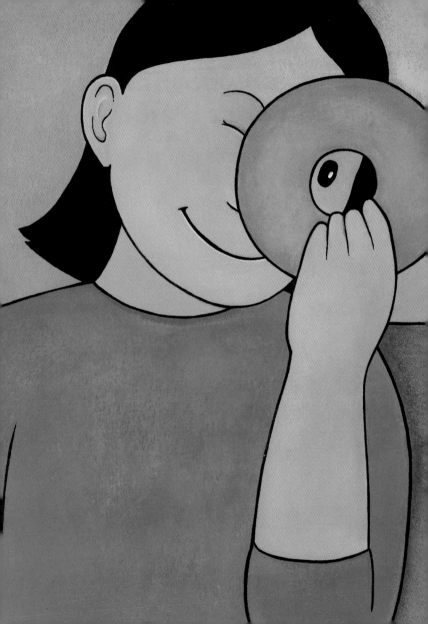

One round doughnut.
One small hole.

One cute puppy.
One very wet kiss.

One soft teddy bear.
One button eye.

One pink pig.
One curly tail.

One birthday cake.
One birthday candle.

One green turtle.
One shell for a home.

One rubber duck.
One clean baby.

One glowing night-light.
One sleeping baby.

One playful kitten.
One ball of yarn to chase.

One gray elephant.
One big sneeze.

One chubby hand.
One favorite rattle.

One little skunk.
One very long white stripe.

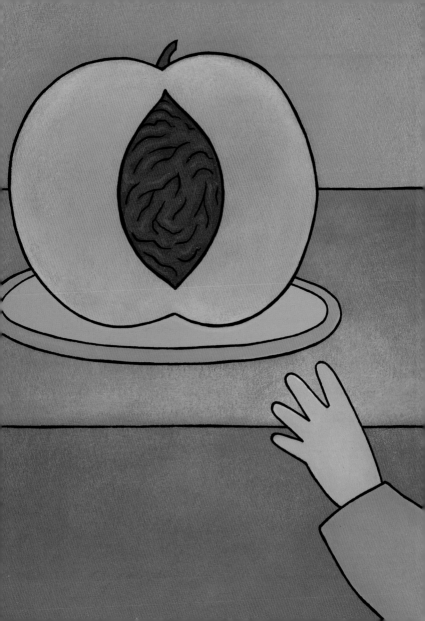

One juicy peach.
One hard pit.

You are very special.
I know that is true.
For when you look
In here,
There's just one you.